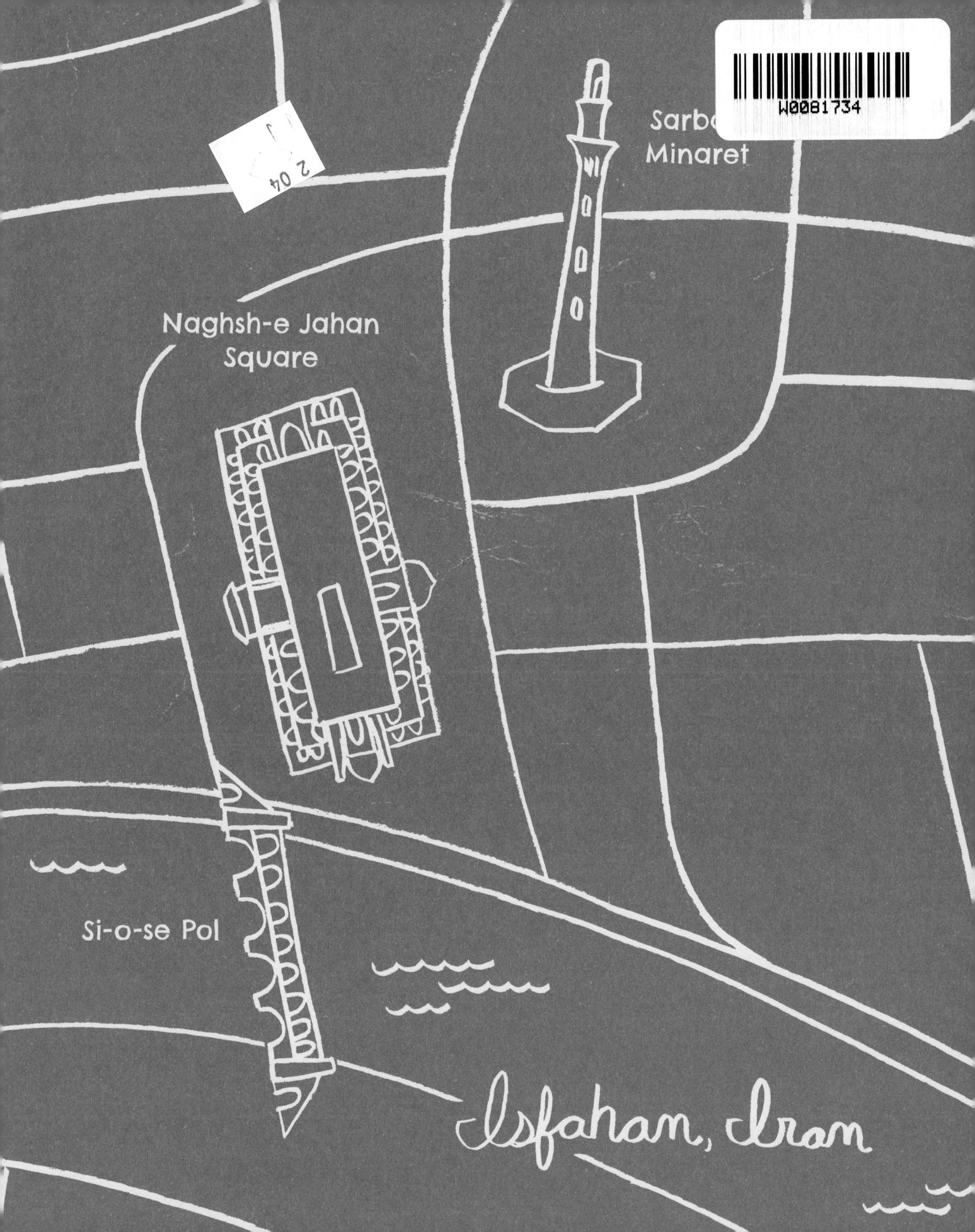

Sarb[...] Minaret

Naghsh-e Jahan Square

Si-o-se Pol

Isfahan, Iran

My Father's House

MINA JAVAHERBIN

illustrated by LINDSEY YANKEY

CANDLEWICK PRESS

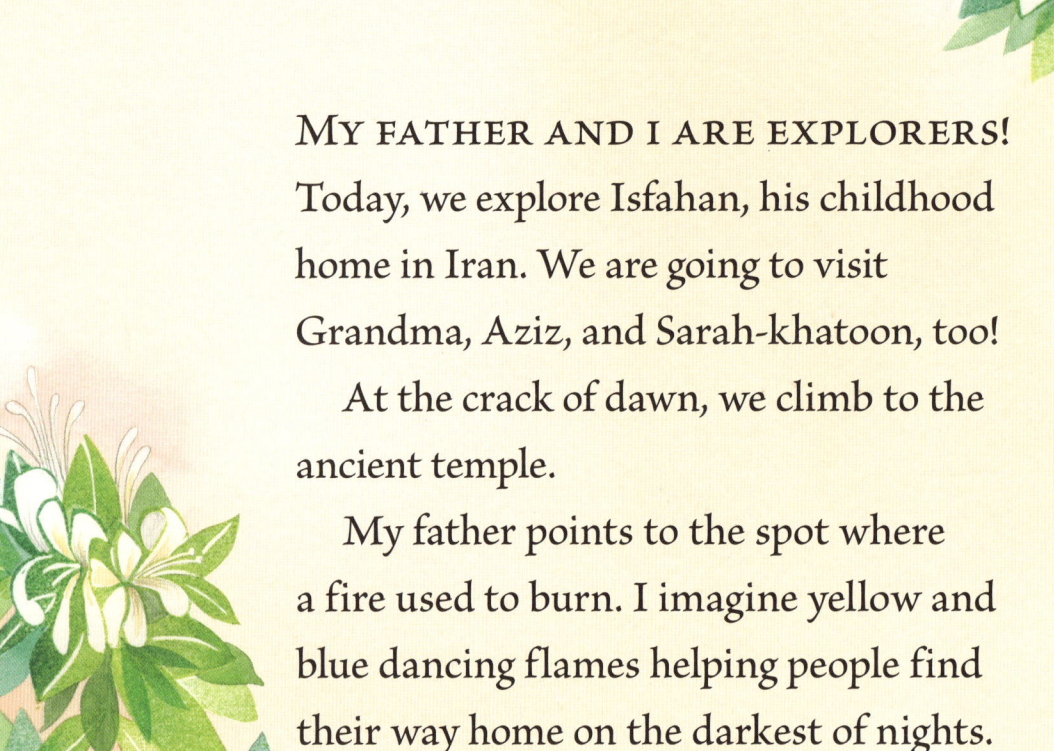

My father and i are explorers! Today, we explore Isfahan, his childhood home in Iran. We are going to visit Grandma, Aziz, and Sarah-khatoon, too!

At the crack of dawn, we climb to the ancient temple.

My father points to the spot where a fire used to burn. I imagine yellow and blue dancing flames helping people find their way home on the darkest of nights.

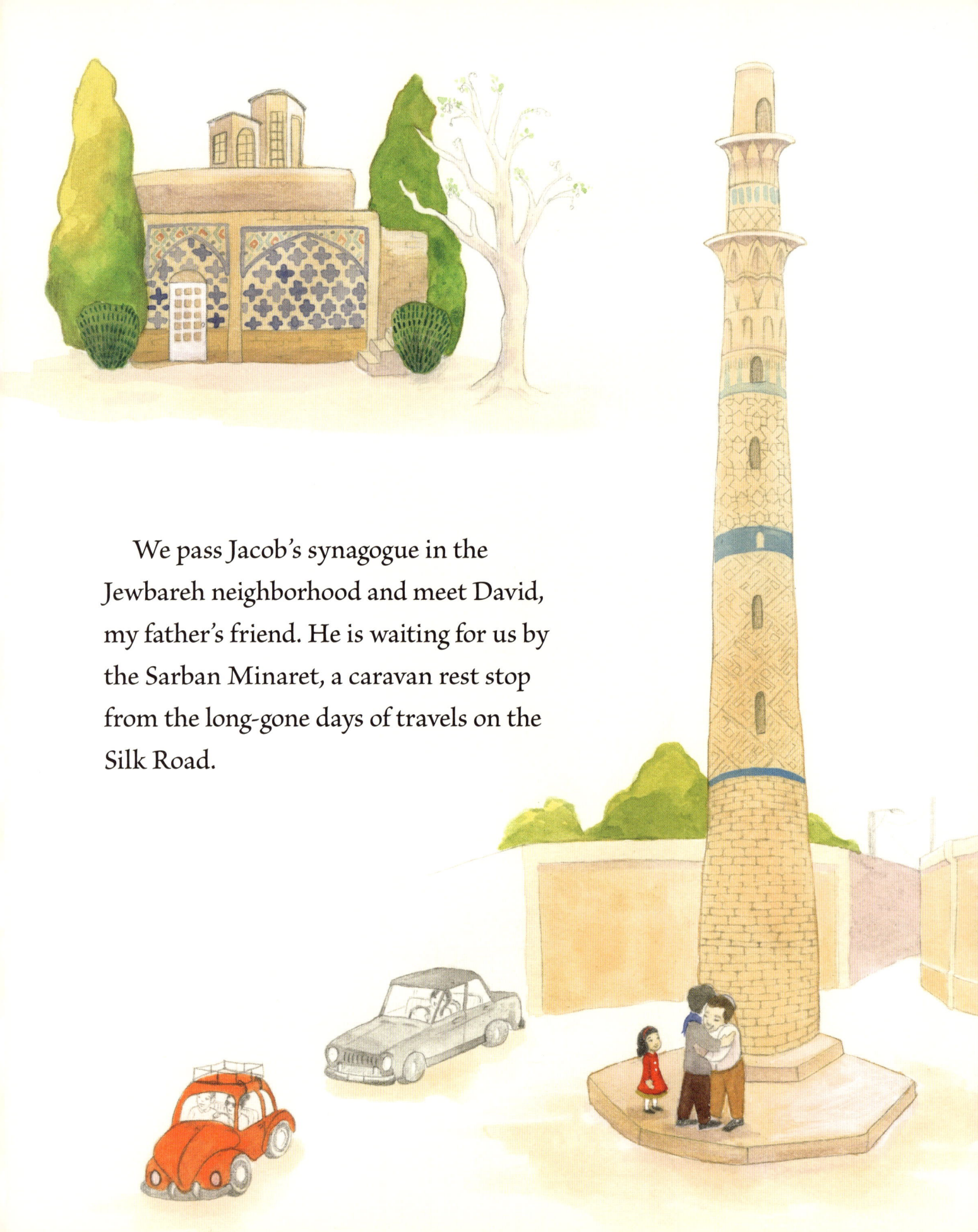

We pass Jacob's synagogue in the Jewbareh neighborhood and meet David, my father's friend. He is waiting for us by the Sarban Minaret, a caravan rest stop from the long-gone days of travels on the Silk Road.

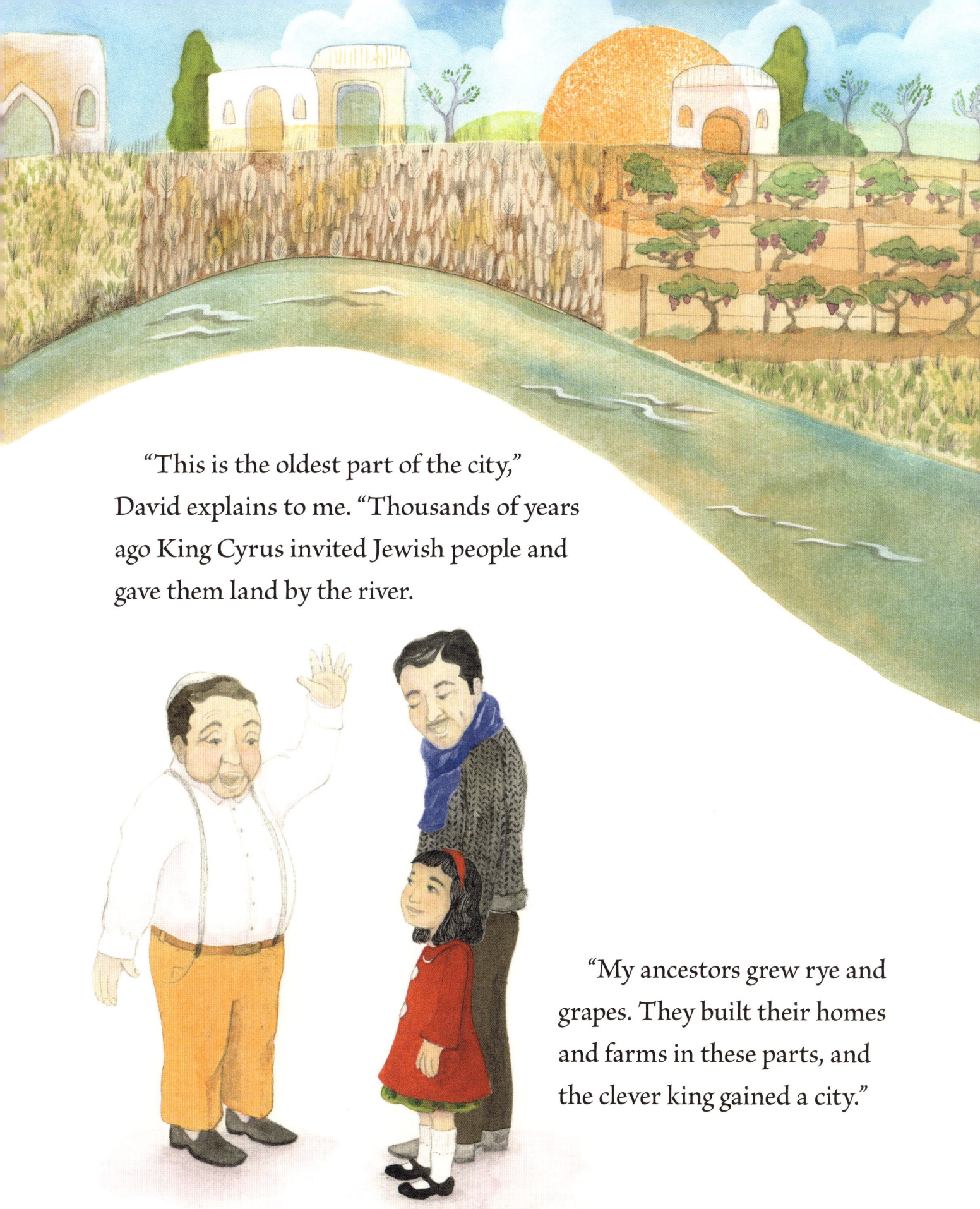

"This is the oldest part of the city," David explains to me. "Thousands of years ago King Cyrus invited Jewish people and gave them land by the river.

"My ancestors grew rye and grapes. They built their homes and farms in these parts, and the clever king gained a city."

Through the old vineyards turned city parks,
we walk to the Julfa neighborhood.

My father and David wave at Vartan, standing in front of
the Vank church. The church was built hundreds of years ago,
when Vartan's ancestors settled here.

Just like when the three were kids, Vartan's mom
has packed them lunch, the best stuffed grape leaves in
the world.

I eat one, two, three, and four. We picnic by the
Si-o-se Pol, a perfect bridge for hide-and-seek, with its
thirty-three arches. After saying goodbye to his friends,
my father is rather quiet. To cheer him up, I count
every arch in my singsong Isfahani accent.

At the city center, my jaw drops! A palace, two mosques,
and the grand bazaar surround the vast pool and gardens.

In the giant square, once a polo field, my father spots
Ali Agha's cart parked by the marble goalposts. He buys us
the fun snack of chickpea flour mixed with powdery sugar.
I picture the galleries around the square teeming with
people of all beliefs. They cheer the players and celebrate
the city they built together, side by side.

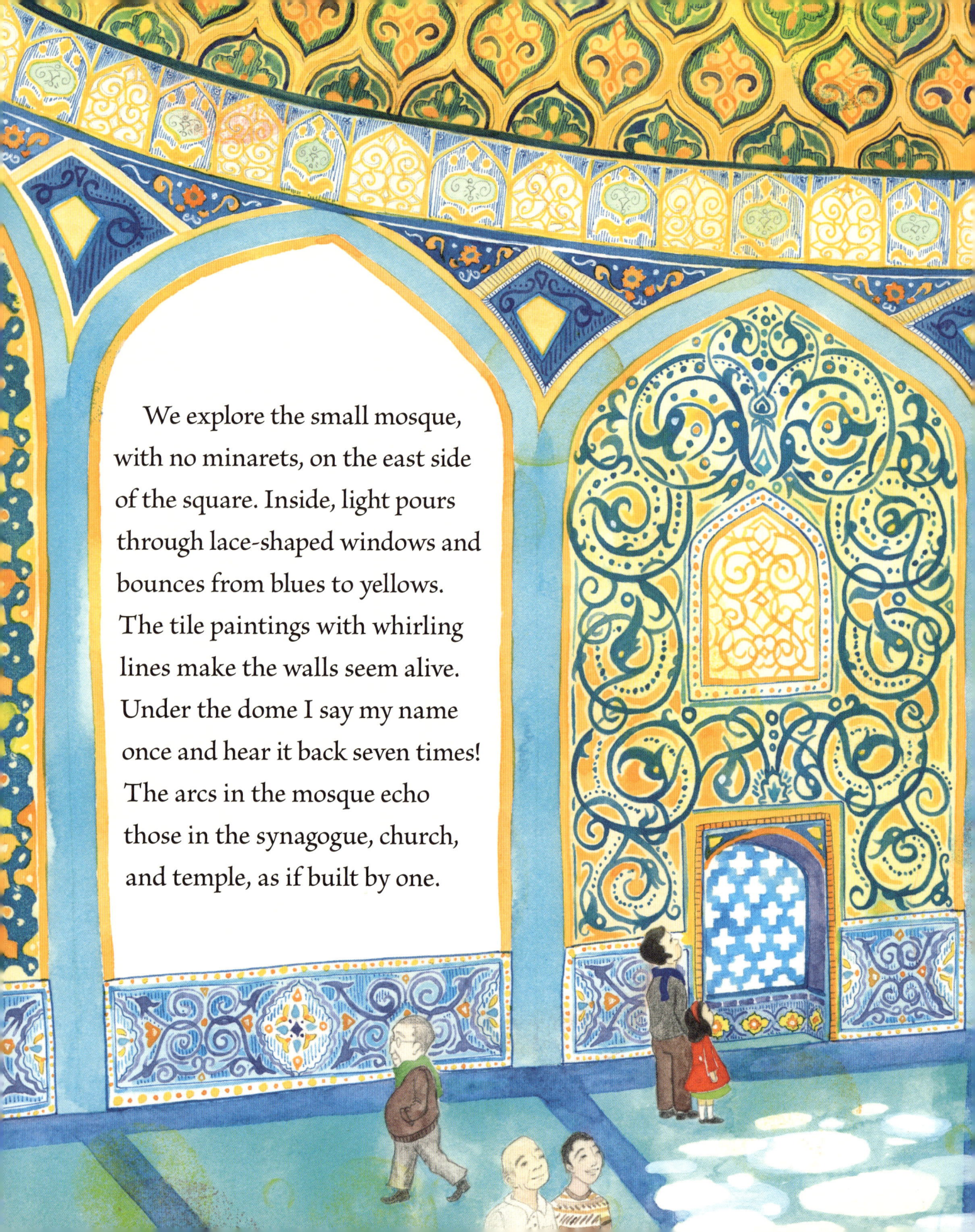

We explore the small mosque, with no minarets, on the east side of the square. Inside, light pours through lace-shaped windows and bounces from blues to yellows. The tile paintings with whirling lines make the walls seem alive. Under the dome I say my name once and hear it back seven times! The arcs in the mosque echo those in the synagogue, church, and temple, as if built by one.

We pass the coppersmith's bazaar, where the hammerings sound like music. We cheerfully skip to my father's house; he hops on a platform by the door. "I used to stand like a statue here and jump up when neighbors walked by."

We play his childhood game and jump when the neighbors walk by. Everyone laughs and plays along, the way they did long ago.

I knock on both doors of my father's house from when he was a boy. The hammer-shaped knocker sounds a thud. The ring one jingles with a zing!

My father's childhood nanny, Sarah-khatoon, arrives home from the bakery. She gives us a piece of fresh sangak bread and tells us to wash up for dinner.

Inside the house, the bright courtyard smells of honeysuckle flowers.

Sangak bread ovens are lined with
small pebbles—some are stuck to the
bread! We wash the pebbles in the pool,
and the nosy fish search for crumbs.

Clink! Clink! The tiny axe echoes under
the terrace arches. Aziz, my father's grandma,
is breaking sugar cones into cubes.

Aziz says, "Pasha! The mortar
is not your bed." He leaps . . .

and comes to me.

With handfuls of sugar, we run to the stables.

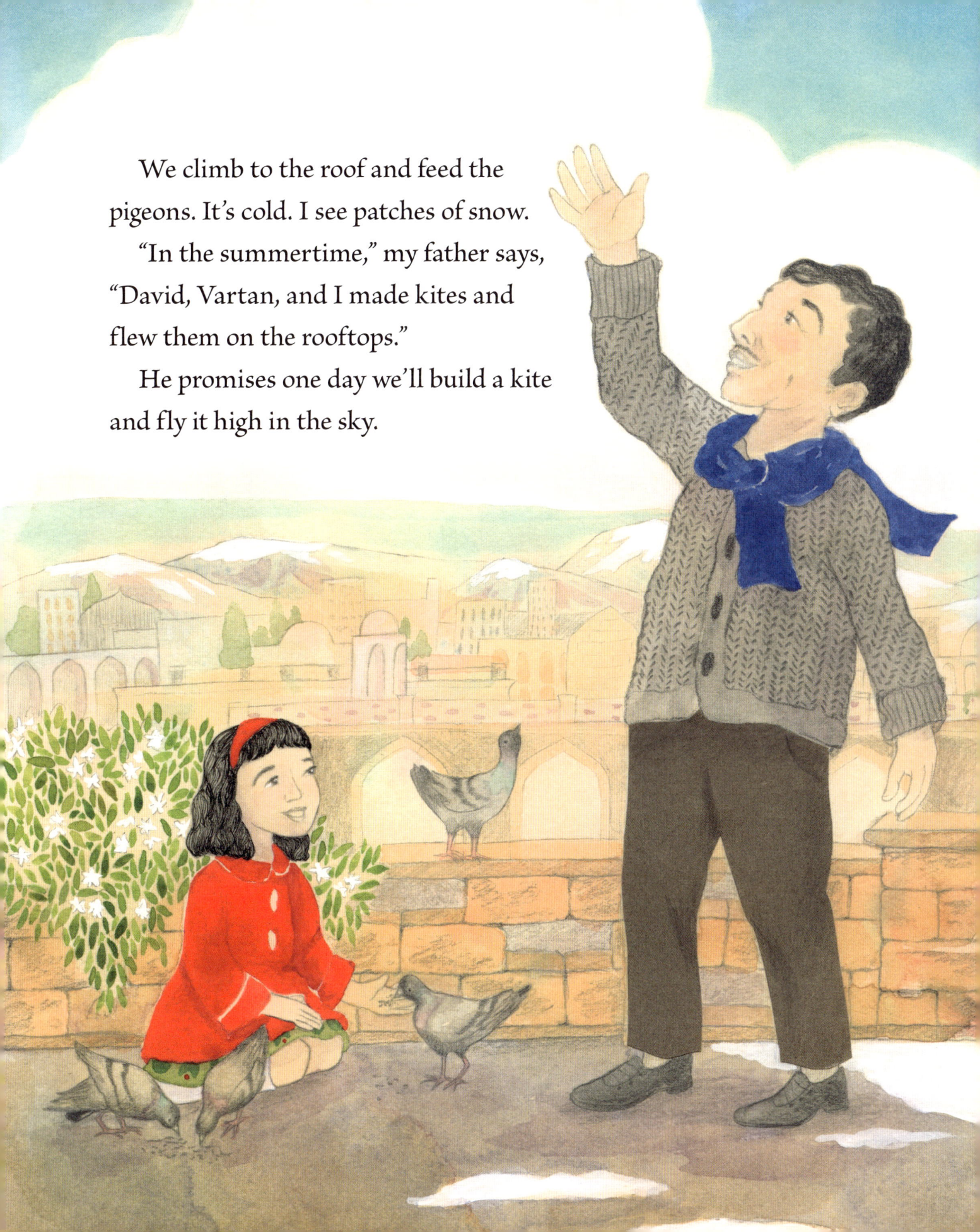

We climb to the roof and feed the pigeons. It's cold. I see patches of snow.

"In the summertime," my father says, "David, Vartan, and I made kites and flew them on the rooftops."

He promises one day we'll build a kite and fly it high in the sky.

We wash by the kitchen pool and offer to carry the trays
upstairs to the shah-neshin room. Aziz and Sarah-khatoon
shoo us out. They say dinner is not ready.

Upstairs, my father slides open an orosi and begins to climb in the room. Grandma, pouring tea from the samovar, gives her son the eye. Father behaves and walks through the door, but Pasha and I jump in. Pasha pounces at the orosi reflections. I give Grandma a hug.

We gather around the large korsi on this cold winter eve. Under the korsi, a metal box holds a few coal embers. Over the korsi, nuts and dried fruit are heaped on large copper trays. Dinner is fesenjān—chicken and rice with walnut-and-pomegranate sauce. Aziz tells us how she changed her pink lamp from oil to electric. My father and I play jacks with the pebbles we saved from the sangak bread.

After dinner, we help clear the dishes with Grandma and Sarah-khatoon.

Pasha falls asleep.

The samovar is emptied, the kitchen is closed, and the pigeons are locked in their coop.

Aziz turns off her antique lamp, and everything falls into darkness.

I snuggle under the soft blankets and dream of
flying kites with my father on the sunny rooftops.

My father and I are explorers.
We go on adventures and stay curious.
He teaches me there is no end to learning
and the world is mine to explore.

He tells me when you bring your own light,
the world becomes your home.

A NOTE FROM THE AUTHOR

The house my father grew up in was located in the city of Isfahan in Iran. People have lived where Isfahan now stands for thousands of years. Ruins of a village on the Fire Temple's hill date back more than three thousand years. Later, when Cyrus the Great took over Babylon, freed the Judeans from slavery, and invited them to live and farm by the Zayandeh River, a town called Yahoudieh gradually formed. People farmed on their homesteads using clever canals engineered to bring water to their crops. These canals are called *maadi*, and they are still a vital feature of modern Isfahan.

When the Sassanids picked a desirable area next to Yahoudieh as a military camp for their army, the population grew. Yahoudieh and the military village merged, and the city's name changed to Ispahan, which means *troops* in Persian, and then to Isfahan. In the centuries that followed, Isfahan became the capital of Persia multiple times. If you take a stroll through the city today, you see evidence of the long-gone eras. From medieval walls and Silk Road minarets to Renaissance palaces, churches, and synagogues, Isfahan has many beautifully made buildings and historical spots, some of which are recognized as World Heritage sites by UNESCO, meaning they are valuable for all of humanity, places to enjoy and keep safe from harm.

My father's house was built in Shahshahan, an aristocratic residential area built on top of flower and agricultural fields seven hundred years ago. In my father's words, "We lived on Baba-noush alley, by Tel Asheghan. Enter bazaar from the square, walk past coppersmith's, through Sineh-Paine to Sonbolestan—our home is right there!"

In many other countries, neighborhoods with this much history are often protected and become tourist destinations, but that isn't the case in Iran. As far as I know, my father's house—like many historical buildings in significant neighborhoods of Isfahan—was neglected and eventually demolished.

The last time my father and I visited his house was in 1972. We left Iran in 1982, along with many other Iranians who chose the hardships of immigration over living under a new oppressive regime. I can never go back to that country and visit only by looking at satellite photos of where I grew up—my school, my street, my city, and my father's house.

GLOSSARY

fesenjān: a winter stew of pheasant or chicken cooked with pomegranate paste and crushed walnuts, served on top of rice

korsi: a low table covered with soft blankets and quilts and set over a small metallic urn containing hot coals. The korsi was used to keep rooms warm in the winter months.

mortar: a kitchen tool used with a pestle to blend and grind, much as food processors are used in modern kitchens

orosi: floor-to-ceiling windows made of light wood and colorful geometric glass. They open vertically; both lower and upper parts are movable to allow one to control the amount of breeze and light. They are arranged in groups of three, five, or seven.

polo: a beloved national sport that originated in Persia and has been occasionally banned and deemed frivolous by various regimes at different points in history

samovar: a large metal kettle used to boil water for tea. The spigot allows for the easy transfer of hot water into the teapot. The top section, where the teapot sits, brews the tea with steam and keeps it warm. Today people still use samovars to make tea, but almost all samovars are run by electricity.

sangak: bread baked in an oven lined with hot river pebbles. Such pebbles were once carried by Persian soldiers to create makeshift ovens for baking bread anywhere.

shah-neshin: the largest and most decorated sitting room in the house, used for receiving guests. Many families also used these beautiful rooms for dining and gathering together.

sugar cones: large loaves of hardened sugar that were cut down into more useful sizes with hammers and crushers. Today most people use factory-made sugar cubes, while sugar cones are reserved for decorative purposes.

To Richard Nelson Frye
MJ

To all the dreamers lighting the way
LY

First edition 2024

Library of Congress Catalog Card Number 2024933805
ISBN 978-1-5362-2553-2

24 25 26 27 28 29 CCP 10 9 8 7 6 5 4 3 2 1

Printed in Shenzhen, Guangdong, China

This book was typeset in Brioso Medium.
The illustrations were done in mixed media.

Candlewick Press
99 Dover Street
Somerville, Massachusetts 02144

www.candlewick.com